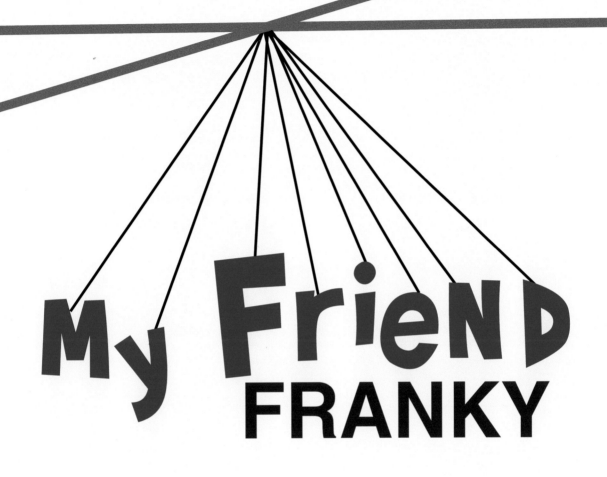

# My FrieND FRANKY

## Written By
# ShelBy Troy
## Illustrated By Kiefer Jenkins

To order additional copies of this book, contact:
Xlibris
1-800-455-039
www.xlibris.com.au
Orders@Xlibris.com.au

Dedicated to Mabel;
who taught me that the
imagination is spectacular!

With Purple hair and orange clothes, a little crazy, so here goes…

My friend Franky was walking down the street, he was skipping along the footpath and whistling with his feet.

Do you whistle with your feet?

Well my friend Franky does,
a great big heap!

5

He went to the supermarket to buy fresh bananas, but went down the wrong aisle and started juggling sultanas!

Do you juggle with sultanas
and whistle with your feet?

Well my friend Franky does,
a great big heap!

He went to the zoo to watch the animals play; the lions were sleeping so he swung around with the monkeys all day.

MONKEY ENCLOSURE

Do you swing around with monkeys, juggle sultanas and whistle with your feet?

Well my friend Franky does, a great big heap!

Before lunch he was thinking about what he should make,

so he took leaves from a tree and made a leaf cake.

Do you make a cake out of leaves, swing around with monkeys, juggle sultanas and whistle with your feet?

Well my friend Franky does, a great big heap!

He likes playing music before going to bed, so started playing the piano with the hair on his head!

Do you play the piano with your hair, make a cake out of leaves, swing around with monkeys, juggle sultanas and whistle with your feet?

Well my friend Franky does, a great big heap!

He went to go make a warm cup of tea, but got so distracted he started an alphabet after Z.

Do you create letters after Z, play the piano with the hair from your head, make a cake out of leaves, swing around with monkeys, juggle sultanas and whistle with your feet?

Well my friend Franky does, a great big heap.

With purple hair and orange clothes, a little crazy…..

well so the story goes…

Printed in the United States
By Bookmasters